NO LIE, PIGS (AND THEIR HOUSES) CAN FLY!

The story of the
THREE LITTLE PIGS

as told by
THE WOLF

by Jessica Gunderson

illustrated by Cristian Bernardini

raintree
a Capstone company — publishers for children

Raintree is an imprint of Capstone Global Library Limited, a company incorporated in England and Wales having its registered office at 7 Pilgrim Street, London, EC4V 6LB – Registered company number: 6695582

www.raintree.co.uk
myorders@raintree.co.uk

Editor: Jill Kalz
Designer: Ted Williams
Creative Director: Nathan Gassman
Production Specialist: Jennifer Walker
The illustrations in this book were created digitally.
Design Elements: Shutterstock: VasilkovS, cover
Printed and bound in China.

ISBN 978 1 4747 1012 1
20 19 18 17 16
10 9 8 7 6 5 4 3 2 1

British Library Cataloguing in Publication Data
A full catalogue record for this book is available from the British Library.

Special thanks to our adviser, Terry Flaherty, PhD, Professor of English, Minnesota State University, Mankato, USA, for his expertise.

Every effort has been made to contact copyright holders of material reproduced in this book. Any omissions will be rectified in subsequent printings if notice is given to the publisher.

All the internet addresses (URLs) given in this book were valid at the time of going to press. However, due to the dynamic nature of the internet, some addresses may have changed, or sites may have changed or ceased to exist since publication. While the author and publisher regret any inconvenience this may cause readers, no responsibility for any such changes can be accepted by either the author or the publisher.

Yep, it's me — the Big Bad Wolf. Now, before you run away or start crying, here's something you should know. And this is the truth. The only thing "big" or "bad" about me is ... well, it's my breath.

Doctors say I have UBS (Uncontrollable Breathing Syndrome). Basically, when I breathe, I let out huge gusts of air. I can't control it. Believe me, I wish I could. It's got me into SO much trouble.

Life with UBS is tough. I breathe out, and rubbish bins tumble down the streets. Trees fall over. On REALLY bad days, aeroplanes teeter off course.

I can't play a good game of football or tennis. Balls shoot into the air, never to be seen again.

"Hey, Wicked Windy!" the other wolves shout. "How's it flying?" Or "Hang on to your hats! Here comes Hurricane Hairy!"

It's a lonely life. That's why I left the pack not long ago, hoping to make new friends.

One day I came upon a straw house in the forest.
A little pig stood inside, stirring a pot of soup. I'd never
known any pigs, but I'd heard they were nice, upstanding
creatures. I thought I might enjoy having a pig as a friend.

I called, **"Little pig, little..."**

WHOOSH!

The house exploded. Straw flew everywhere.

The startled pig took one look at me
and jumped ... right into the boiling pot
of soup.

Wanting to apologize, I peeked into the pot. No pig!
Just a fat, juicy ham. I took a few bites. Delicious!
That pig, wherever he was, could certainly make a good soup.

Further into the forest, I came upon a house made of wood. A little pig stood inside, frying potatoes over a fire.

I called, **"Little pig, little pig, let..."**

CRASH!

The wood house splintered into hundreds of pieces. The surprised pig saw me and leapt ... straight into the hot frying pan.

I was so sorry for blowing down the pig's house. I wanted to apologize. But when I peered into the pan ... there was no pig in sight. Just strips of sizzling bacon.

Yummy!

Finally I came to a house made of bricks. A little pig stood inside, stirring a pot of stew.

"Little pig, little pig, let me in!" I called. (Guess what? The house didn't move!)

The pig saw me and shouted, "Not by the hair of my chinny chin chin!"

Maybe he had heard about the other pigs' houses and the messes I'd made. I needed to do something nice. So I gathered a basket of turnips and apples. The pig opened the door, grabbed the treats and slammed the door.

My stomach growled. I hoped the pig would share his stew with me and we could be friends. I knocked, but he didn't answer. So I scampered up the wall and wriggled through the chimney.

Not clever.

WHOOP! I fell right into the pot of boiling stew.
"AAHHH!" I shrieked.

"You've ruined my supper!" the pig cried.

But then he giggled.

"Goodness, look at you," he said. "With your fur all burnt, you look like a pig."

I did look awfully pink.

"I'm sorry I was unkind earlier," said the pig (whose name was Mortar; Mort for short). "Wolves don't usually want to be friends with pigs. They usually want to eat them."

I told Mort about my UBS and how the other wolves bullied me about it.

"Have you ever tried using it for good?" he asked.

"What do you mean?" I asked.

"Follow me, I'll show you."

Mort led me to a little blue house. Inside, a girl was huffing and puffing, trying to blow out her birthday candles. Mort nudged me. I leant through the window and blew. The candles went out, and all the children cheered.

Later we found a group of children trying to fly their kites. The day was calm, and the kites wouldn't move. But when I breathed in their direction, the kites sailed into the air.

So that's my story. Mort and I have become good friends. And his house is so sturdy, I never worry about blowing it down by accident. He made some stew again tonight. "No meat in here?" I asked.

"I don't eat meat," he said.

"Not even bacon?"

Mort shook his head and sighed. "No, Wolf, not even bacon. Not even when pigs fly!"

Discussion points

Look in your local library or online to find the classic version of "The Three Little Pigs". Describe how the character of the wolf looks and acts. Compare and contrast him with the wolf in this version of the story.

At first the third pig, Mort, doesn't want to be friends with the wolf. What events cause Mort to change his mind?

If Mort told the story instead of the wolf, what details might he tell differently? What if the first pig, who lived in the straw house, told the story? How would his point of view differ?

Glossary

character person, animal or creature in a story
plot what happens in a story
point of view way of looking at something
version account of something from a certain
    point of view

Read more

Fairy Tales (Writing Stories), Anita Ganeri
(Raintree, 2014)

The Empty Pot (Folk Tales From Around the World),
Charlotte Guillain (Raintree, 2014)

The Three Little Wolves and the Big Bad Pig,
Eugene Trivizas (Egmont, 2015)

Website

www.bbc.co.uk/education/clips/zyx2tfr

An exploration of one of the great mysteries of our
time - why did the first of the three little pigs choose
to build a house from straw?

Look out for all the books in this series:

Believe Me, Goldilocks Rocks!

Believe Me, I Never Felt a Pea!

Frankly, I'd Rather Spin Myself a New Name!

Frankly, I Never Wanted to Kiss Anybody!

Honestly, Red Riding Hood Was Rotten!

No Kidding, Mermaids Are a Joke!

No Lie, I Acted Like a Beast!

No Lie, Pigs (and Their Houses) CAN Fly!

Really, Rapunzel Needed a Haircut!

Seriously, Cinderella Is SO Annoying!

Seriously, Snow White Was SO Forgetful!

Truly, We Both Loved Beauty Dearly!

Trust Me, Hansel and Gretel Are SWEET!

Trust Me, Jack's Beanstalk Stinks!